THE PSYCHIC DETECTIVE

A WILKINSON'S DETECTIVE AGENCY SHORT STORY

ALEXANDRIA BLAELOCK

Also by Alexandria Blaelock

THE PSYCHIC DETECTIVE

A WILKSINSON'S DETECTIVE AGENCY SHORT STORY

ALEXANDRIA BLAELOCK

BlueMere Books
MELBOURNE, AUSTRALIA

For permission requests, please contact enquiries@bluemerebooks.com.

Ordering Information:
Discounts are available on quantity purchases. For details, contact orders@bluemerebooks.com.

The Psychic Detective/Alexandria Blaelock
paperback ISBN: 978-1-922744-63-0
digital ISBN: 978-1-922744-64-7

Book Layout © BookDesignTemplates.com
Cover Art © Volodymyr Nikulin/Depositphotos

BlueMere Books
www.bluemerebooks.com

THE PSYCHIC DETECTIVE

Derek Ericsson slumped at his desk, situated in the centre of a sea of grey cubicles in the northeast quadrant of the floor his soulless, heartless employer occupied.

Furthest from the convenience of the toilets, and the kitchens, but not far enough from the aromas drifting through the ventilation shafts.

Derek was in his forties, his balding pate inadequately concealed by his comb-over, with not nearly enough courage to shave his head and be done with it.

It was after six, and there was next to no one left in the office. He risked ducking down behind his desk to take a shot of vodka from the water bottle he'd decanted it into, and popped a mint in his mouth on the way up.

His bitch of a thirty-something overachieving boss would sack him on the spot if she knew about the day drinking.

And then he would be forced to stay home with his demon spawn children. Lucy aged three, T—

and Peter aged twelve.

As usual, he winced as he almost named Thomas. Beautiful, angelic Tommy who would have been ten this year, had he not been mown down on the sidewalk outside their home by a drunk driver when he was six.

Derek was haunted by the nameless, faceless driver who had never been found.

Lucy was his wife's replacement child.

Somehow, she'd moved on, leaving him behind.

But he just couldn't get past Tommy, the light of his life, now cold and alone in death.

"Derek, Derek, Derek," she who shall remain nameless dropped down to his level in a cloud of some kind of musky perfume.

"What am I going to do with you?"

Derek slumped even lower, the picture of misery.

She put her palm on his shoulder and pushed him upright, "you know Wilkinson's won't stand for this."

He refused to meet her eyes or say anything.

"Derek," she shook his shoulder, "look, I like you. You're reliable, and the best analyst in my team. I would hate to lose you."

He risked looking up at her, to see her face full of compassion.

A tear leaked from his eye and fell on her knee.

She shook his shoulder again, gentler this time, "you have to get your shit together. I won't be able to hide it forever."

Another tear dropped, though his face remained passive and still.

"Take a month off. See someone."

She stepped away and he heard her rummaging through a draw in her desk by the window.

In a few moments, she was back, pressing a crumpled business card into his hand, "see her. She'll help. Now go."

He dropped the card in his pocket without looking at it and scrambled to pick up his briefcase and leave before she changed her mind.

He risked looking back at the door as he left, "call her," she shouted, "I'll let her know to expect your call."

And then he scuttled away as fast as he could.

《《 • 》》

Shirley Weaving, Private Investigator was at that moment enjoying an animated debate with Great Uncle Edward Weaving, her spirit guide about the relative merits of the old or new Magnum, and therefore which one to watch that evening.

Obviously, there was a clear divide between the living and the dead. They needed a circuit breaker, but then again, they often did.

Great Uncle Edward had insisted she take the old heritage-listed building with the grand façade, in a leafy main street of an older, well established southeastern suburb of Melbourne.

It was one of 25 shops running around the corner, along two sides of a large park.

Originally, shops had lined both streets, but these were all that remained, with larger modern constructions replacing the old before the heritage listing came through.

She, on the other hand, had been keen on the stark, ultra-modern office with the hip inner-city location.

But, she had to agree the location he'd chosen was delightful.

Her shop sat opposite the statue and garden commemorating the war dead, with a view through to the local sports ground.

The balcony of the flat above the shop had a good view of community activities all year round.

The shop front had beautiful stained-glass panels along the top, bottom and sides of the full-length picture windows. The wooden floorboards creaked reassuringly as she walked on them.

And her collection of random second-hand furniture collected from rubbish dumps and council collections somehow looked satisfyingly right in situ.

There was an excellent Chinese restaurant at one end of one leg, the post office at the other, and a magnificent bakery more or less in the middle. Not to mention a delicious café, small continental butcher, and an organic produce store. All the necessities of life nearby.

Within a five-minute walk of the tram terminus, and twenty minutes from the train station.

It was entirely possible Great Uncle Edward preferred this location as there was a "better" quality of ghost neighbours than the inner-city-working-class location.

The elderly owner died shortly after she moved in, and conveniently, the estate gave her the option to purchase the freehold.

She hated to say he was right, but she had to admit there was something slow and satisfying about the location, and her particular line of detective services flourished here.

Not that she made a big deal about that.

The day had been one of those slow days, the kind she usually associated with the calm before the storm. As if some beneficent entity gave her a quiet day to build her strength.

She'd caught up with all her filing, sent reminders for the overdue accounts, and in a burst of vanity, even cleaned the brass business plaque fixed on the pillar beside the door.

All the outstanding activities were taken care of, and there was nothing left to do.

She'd gratefully closed and locked the door, and climbed the wooden stairs to her apartment come storage unit above the office.

Once there, she opened a bottle of Cabernet Sauvignon, microwaved some leftover Chinese and opened a dialogue about whether to watch the old or new *Magnum P.I.*.

Edward had to be convinced, if not, he simply cut the power. As he'd done with *John Wick*, claiming it wasn't suitable viewing for a young woman.

She'd been forced to watch it at her friend Gabrielle's place and had conveniently forgotten the small brick fragment she generally carried to permit him to visit locations with her.

"Someone's coming," he said, breaking into her point of Magnum proof.

She dropped her hand, letting the remote fall to the floor as she turned to look towards the window overlooking the park.

Not that she could see the street from the flat upstairs, but she could feel a tangled mess of black, orange and red moving along the sidewalk toward her. Its cold, sucking energy seemed to draw her in, and Edward put his hand on her shoulder to hold her steady.

"Whatever that is," she said, "is like a black hole sucking all the life and energy of everything around it into itself."

He grunted in agreement, "perhaps some kind of grief eating monster."

She snapped her fingers, and a halo of gold-tipped white and yellow sprang up around her.

"It's right outside the shop," he said, gripping her shoulder more firmly.

They watched it looking in the office for a while before it turned and walked back the way it had come.

She let the halo dissipate and flopped onto the couch, "I'm exhausted!"

Edward sat beside her and grunted in agreement, "I wonder if that was the Ericsson guy Gabrielle called about."

"I'd say so. She said we'd know what to do when he got here."

"Some kind of exorcism?"

ALEXANDRIA BLAELOCK

"Well," she let out a sigh, "I can already tell there's some massive thing eating away at him, but until we meet him, I won't know what it's going to take to strip it away."

"No...

"I think maybe I might need to ask around my fellow guides..."

She took advantage of his preoccupation to start watching the new Magnum. When he realised, the lights started flickering, but then he subsided to the couch and enjoy the show.

The next morning, she prepared for the visit of the owner of the black aura by burning clove oil to purify the space, calm the owner and enhance her gifts.

She filled up the coffee machine ready to go, put the kettle on in case he wanted tea, and opened a fresh packet of chocolate biscuits.

As part of her preparation routine, she put on *Never Mind the Bollocks, Here's the Sex Pistols*, and jacked up the volume. Jumping, headbanging and dancing to dissipate the stress and tension that had been building since the visitation last night.

And to prevent it from getting worse.

What could the owner of such negative vibes need with her services?

Shirley was a fully licensed Private Investigator, and did all the usual kind of

8

investigations; background checks, computer and phone forensics, missing persons, surveillance.

It was just, well, she had outside help.

So far out, it was from the Other Side.

From Great Uncle Edward.

Who added an unearthly dimension to the investigations.

She felt it approaching again and allowed the fear to shift her perception a little higher, before turning to look out the window.

Without her third eye, she would have seen a perfectly ordinary white, middle-aged man. Receding hairline, expanding waistline, bowed and exhausted by the weight of something.

With her third eye, she could see the monster he was carrying on his back. An awful, ugly, bloated monster. It looked kind of like a diseased, bloated corpse, crossed with an insanely large slug whose rows of sharp teeth were firmly locked on his neck.

No wonder he looked kind of wasted and greyed out with the weight of the monster.

"I don't know why I'm here," he said as she opened the door for him.

A crackle of energy heralded the arrival of Edward, "what in the name of all that's holy is that thing?"

<I'm not sure,> she thought back.

As if the creature knew it was talking about it, it kind of twisted its head without moving and focused its small and beady eyes on them.

<What the fuck!> she thought.

"Indeed," Edward said, and after a short pause, as if he'd just realised, "language!"

"Why don't you come in and tell me about it," she said, taking a step back and indicating a translucent folding screen with an oriental pattern, behind which a couple of cosy chairs were visible, but obscured.

"Sure," he said and moved forward. He looked as though it was taking a lot of effort as if he was walking waist-deep through water.

She tried to keep her face impassive as the creature appeared to be trying to make him turn around and walk out again.

"Here sit down," she said, "would you like something to drink? Tea? Coffee? Water?"

The creature recoiled, as though something had poked it. It writhed around on the man's neck, and somehow, pulled itself inside the man's body.

It seemed the clove oil was working, though not exactly in the way she'd intended.

"Coffee please. I feel like I need the kick."

Edward turned the machine on, and the man turned to look at it.

"It's on a timer. Milk and sugar?"

"Milk and two sugars," he replied.

She'd previously noticed people relaxed when they watched a woman bustle in a kitchen, so she asked, "why don't you tell me what's bothering you while I make it?"

He slumped in an armchair and sank into himself.

"My name's Derek Ericsson."

Definitely Gabrielle's guy.

She knew the nub of the matter now, dead child, and it looked like the monster was feeding off Derek's grief.

Nonetheless, she made a questioning encouraging noise, as she walked to the kitchen where he watched her grab a couple of mugs from a wall cabinet.

She let him talk, occasionally encouraging him to continue as she put the biscuits on a plate and brought them over. And then returned with the coffee. And then sat down next to him.

"I'm guessing that you'd like me to find the driver of the car?"

"Yes," he said, the most decisive thing he'd said.

The creature lunged out of his neck, but as it met the clove oil suspended in the atmosphere, retreated again almost instantly.

"I will certainly do my best, but it's been four years, so I'm not sure what I'll be able to achieve."

Derek smiled. Just a small smile, but his face showed a tiny sign of hope.

"Thank you. I know there's a one in a million chance, but I just don't know where to start looking."

The creature popped its head out and glared at her.

"You've given me a location, and a date and time of death, and that's a start."

Derek pulled out of his slump, and sat straighter in the chair, "how will you move on?"

"I'm not sure exactly, probably start with the police report, talk to your wife and any witnesses."

"No one came forward at the time."

"Not to worry, sometimes things like this weigh on people, and after a while, they feel the need to unburden themselves."

He smiled a straight lipped smile, "I suppose they do. Look at me here, after all this time, trying to find out."

"Quite so. What will you do in the meantime?"

"I've been feeling tired and suicidal. As though I just can't take it anymore. But now, I feel like I can breathe at last. As though I've taken the first step towards something significant."

"Just hold onto that thought for a moment."

She went back to the cupboard under the stairs, "something for grief," she said, as if she was thinking.

Edward picked out a piece of raw obsidian.

She passed it through the haze of clove oil the burner was emitting, and brought it back to Derek.

"Take this piece of obsidian, and when you feel yourself sliding back, take it out and turn it around and around in your hand."

He took it, dropped it as if it was hot, and scrambled to find it and pick it up again. "I'm sorry, I don't know how it fell through my fingers!"

Shirley could see the creatures head coming out of Derek's neck as far as it dared, glaring at her. So, once he'd grabbed it again, she reached out and folded her hands around his.

"It's going to be okay. We're going to get through this."

He smiled hesitantly, and she could see a small piece of him was ready to return to living. He let his hands stay in hers for a moment, and then put the stone in his pocket and stood up.

"Shall I call back next week to see how it's going?"

"Of course. I'll definitely have something for then."

She took a step back freeing the path towards the door, not wanting to get any closer to the monster.

Derek left, standing a little taller and freeer than when he'd arrived. He paused at the door, the creature struggling to expand beyond his body again, but left without saying another word.

The first step was to call her friend Jeremy, at the Department of Justice about the Police case file.

"You know I can't just look up the system - it tracks all the access requests against the Freedom of Information file numbers. But if the case is still unsolved after four years, chances are it's available.

"Send me the FOI request and I'll get onto it straight away."

The next step was to take Edward with her to look at the crime scene.

It was one of the newer subdivisions, with roundabouts and other traffic calming devices. Given the address, she could see the driver must have driven straight over the roundabout and mounted the curb on the other side.

By the look of it, the incident could have been a lot worse. The house was at the minimum distance from the kerb, and without a fence they were lucky.

The car could have taken out the kid, and half the front of the house as well.

<Are there any entities around here?> she asked him telepathically.

"Nothing obvious," he said, "but there's something here. I suppose you can feel it.

<Definitely something,> she rotated on the spot, looking in all directions. She felt itchy, like every millimetre of skin was bitten by mosquitoes.

<Feels like it's coming from across the road,> she scratched her arm.

"Mmm."

She rotated to the right, a bit to the left, and then right again until she was looking at an undeveloped two-story house within a garden consisting of builder's rubble.

A curtain twitched.

Edward was over there in an instant, "there's a woman here, she has one of those worm things attached to her neck."

<I'll be there in a sec,> she said, applying some clove oil diluted with unscented hand cream to her hands and arms as she strolled over to the house.

She knocked on the door, and nothing happened within the house.

"She won't answer," Shirley turned to see a plump, middle-aged woman hanging over the fence.

"Why not?"

"Her daughter died about four years ago."

Shirley turned toward Edward standing by the front door; he shrugged his shoulders.

"Yes," the woman continued, "just after they moved in. Leukaemia it was. Poor Mrs Andrews never got over it."

Shirley turned back towards the woman, "actually, I'm a private investigator hired by Mr Ericsson to look into his son's death," she pulled out her license for the woman to check. "Did the Andrew's girl die around the same time?"

The woman looked at the card, thought for a while, then handed it back. "Yes, it was around the same time. June that year was a really bad month.

"And as well as those two kids, there was the Jackson girl at number 22 from an accident at the recreational centre, the Lee boy at 23 drowned in their swimming pool, and Miss Dine's new puppy at 24.

"Bit Mr Singh at number 25 and had to be put down. I don't think they've spoken to each other since then."

Edward appeared behind the woman, giving Shirley a hard look.

"So, six houses clustered close by," she said, looking back at him, "that's dreadful! Surely not all on the same day?"

"Oh no, pretty much the same as I said. Ericsson was first, the next day the Andrews' girl, the next day Jackson, then Lee, then the puppy incident, then the puppy was euthanised."

"Five deaths in six days? That doesn't make sense."

"No-no, five deaths in five days. Now that I think about it, that's quite shocking. I suppose that's the benefit of time."

There was something nudging at the back of Shirley's mind, and she couldn't tell whether keeping the woman talking would spill it over into her consciousness and send it further away.

"Were you here the day Thomas Ericsson died?"

"Oh yes, I run the local childcare co-op, so I'm always here. I didn't see the accident, but I heard the thud. Someone started screaming, and the car backed up and drove away. Miracle the car started.

"They found what was left of it on the vacant ground for the new subdivision in Charles Street. Burnt out wreck apparently. They just towed the car away and started the construction." The woman shuddered luxuriously, "I wouldn't want to be living in that house I can tell you."

"So you didn't see anything?"

"No one saw anything. Considering the screaming, it was so strange. No one saw anything when any of the children died. It was like some kind of demonic intervention." She shuddered again.

The sound of children screaming came from inside the house.

"I'd best be getting back," she said, turning away, "good luck with your investigations. That family could really do with some good luck."

<I'm getting the feeling there should be more deaths,> she thought to Edward.

"I feel like there should be at least another two."

<Do you think all the families have these things in their necks?>

"Grief slugs? We're two for two with Mrs Andrews."

<Should we check the other families?>

"Yes. I really think we should."

Shirley paused to put more clove oil hand cream on her hands and arms, then walked to the next house in the street.

They visited numbers 22 through to 25, ostensibly searching for evidence to do with the

Ericsson matter, but really looking for more evidence of grief slugs.

And they found it in all the houses except Derek Ericsson's

"Oh, I made him move out a couple of years ago," Mrs Ericsson said, "he was bringing the whole family down with his relentless Tommy this and Tommy that."

Edward gave her a hard look.

"I'm sorry if this seems insensitive," Shirley said, "but weren't you affected by Thomas' death?"

Mrs Ericsson sighed. "Yes. It was very hard at the time.

"But my son, Peter was hurting just as much, if not more than Derek, and he just couldn't see it. I didn't want Peter's life to be overshadowed by Thomas' death.

"And then Lucy came along, and I didn't have the time to dwell on Thomas anymore. Lucy deserved two fully functioning parents, but one was better than none.

"Actually, it was Thomas' birthday the other day, and we went to the cemetery to visit him."

"I see," Shirley replied.

What was it about Derek that the grief slug could overwhelm his defences when his wife and son could fight it off?

"Why do you think he couldn't move on from the death of his son?" she asked

Mrs Ericsson thought about it for a while, "because he's always gone all-in on everything - it's his nature to overachieve. Though I couldn't say where it came from."

"I see."

"Look, I'd love to chat more; there's something about you that makes it easy, but the kids will be home soon, and I need to get ready.

"Tell Derek to get his shit together, and come back home to where he belongs."

"I will," Shirley said, and watched the woman walk away.

You couldn't get more of a contrast between the two of them. She was fit and vibrant, he was anything but. She was calm and confident, while he was bowed beneath the weight of the grief slug.

<We have to figure out where the grief slugs came from, and how to kill them.>

"I couldn't agree with you more."

Shirley walked back to the street and looked up and down.

<Could the slugs be something that was here already, or was it introduced?>

Edward shrugged, "beats me. Let's go home and do some research."

Back in the office, she mixed up some lemon, cypress and rosemary essential oils for focus and concentration, and lit the oil burner.

And he disappeared, presumably to check his spirit sources about the monster.

She sat on the couch, crossed her legs, and started researching slugs on her laptop. Not that she knew it was a slug, but it was somewhere to start.

Before long, she'd uncovered two possible methods of transfer.

Some slugs transmit genetic material through darts they fire at other slugs.

Other slugs leave clutches of up to 30 eggs deposited somewhere damp, like under a rock or log. Where they lay dormant until the conditions are right for them to hatch.

To be honest, the dart was her favourite, but given most parasites breed in the soil and are transmitted by skin contact, it seemed more likely that was the method of transfer.

So.

As a new subdivision, it was possible a grief slug egg cache was already there, ready to be disturbed during the construction phase.

But it was more or less equally possible, some kind of carrier had visited each of the houses on subsequent days. Someone like a council inspector certifying occupancy.

Ah, but it was after they moved in, so not the council. Could the builder have sent someone to catalogue or fix construction faults?

She needed to know more about the car that killed the Ericsson boy.

In a rare moment of synchronicity, the phone rang. She pulled it out of her pocket; it was Jeremy.

"I'll post the documents out to you, but the vehicle was registered to Jeff Dawson, who claimed it had been stolen the night before. Guess who he worked for?"

"Would it be QPY Construction?"

"Oh my god! Every time! Post-construction follow up."

She laughed, "I was out at the site investigating this morning."

"Ah. Well, I bet you can't guess what happened to Jeff Dawson after the crash."

"He died?"

"Again? Bet you don't know how."

"I don't, but I'd be interested to find out."

"Suicide. It seems his wife and child were hit by a train a year or so before the Ericsson case, and he hadn't got over it."

Edward reappeared in the office and started talking.

"Shhh-it," she said, making a quelling motion, "he suicided? How?"

"Crashed his car. Is it possible he decided spur of the moment to drive headfirst into the Ericsson house, not realising the boy was right in front of him?"

"Crashed his car?" she said looking at Edward, who nodded, "I imagine it's possible. Likely even. What did the Police report say?"

"They didn't interview him; he died the day before they contacted him. That's why the investigation closed - couldn't prove it either way."

"Thanks so much Jeremy, I owe you."

"Sure do, what about some of those strudels with the extra cloves?"

"Next time you're here?"

"It's a date. Then you can tell me all about your case."

"Sure thing. I'll see ya."

"Not if I see ya first," he cackled, and hung up before she could get a comment in.

She threw the phone down, stood up and stretched, "I have so much to tell you," she said to Edward.

"And I you, but you go first."

She filled him in on slug reproduction, including the dart method. Then about the driver visiting each of the houses and potentially transmitting the slugs.

And then her theory, that if they didn't get rid of the Ericsson slug, it would drive him to suicide shortly.

"Well, he did mention it was all getting too much for him, and he wished he was dead," Edward said.

"At least we can tell him who was responsible for his son's death to put his mind at ease. But if we can't kill the slug, I think it will kill him. And presumably send out slug darts to those in the vicinity as it dies."

"Yes," Edward said. "What about the cloves - the oil in the burner made it pull itself back into Ericsson's body. Can you administer it orally?"

"Actually yes. Jeremy was asking for some apple strudel. I could make a batch with too many cloves in it. That ought to be enough to drive it out of Ericsson's body."

"So sweet," said Edward, making a heart shape with his fingers and resting his chin on them.

Shirley made a face at him, "all that's left then, is figuring out a way of killing the grief slug when it's exposed. Something easily transferable to the other families."

"Interesting conundrum," said Edward, "how do you kill a creature no one can see?

"I don't know much about grief slugs *per se*, but you can kill ordinary slugs with coffee, beer, vinegar, cornmeal, ammonia, garlic, ash, and copper."

"Or is there some kind of bird or frog-like monster predator or slug parasite we could use?"

"Chickens love slugs. And chickens have ultraviolet vision, so it's possible they could see the slugs."

"You know who has chickens?" Shirley asked, "the Singh's have chickens. That might be why Mr Singh didn't catch the slugs. I wonder if they'd let us borrow one?"

"No need, Edna a couple of doors down has some."

"Right," said Shirley, counting on her fingers, "apple strudel to drive it out, and a chicken to kill it. Shall we call Ericsson?"

"I think sooner is better than later, but what if we can't contain the monster?"

"You raise a valid point, but I don't think we can afford to wait. We could try a mix of patchouli and bergamot to relax the emotion centres and promote emotional balance."

"Okay, let's do it. Though I don't know that I can do anything to protect you if this goes wrong."

"We'll worry about that later."

She called him, and he agreed to visit the next day.

The next day, she made their preparations; the oils in the burner, the coffee and strudel, the Sex Pistols, and the chicken, contained in a pen with a handful of corn.

When Derek arrived, she was waiting with the coffee and strudel.

The slug seemed smaller, and he seemed less bent and more capable, so she guessed he'd turned a corner.

He tucked into his snack as they talked about the weather and other inconsequentialities.

The slug wasn't happy, roiling on his neck as though it had a stomach ache. Not too much; it seemed the oils were doing a good job of anaesthetising it.

Suddenly the chicken broke through its pen and made a rush at the slug, leaping through the air and scratching it off Derek's neck in passing.

He brushed his neck, not noticing the blood, watching in fascination as the bird appeared to be rolling on its back and shaking its head like a cat with a toy.

"Is your chicken okay? It seems to be having a fit."

"I'm sure it's fine. I hope it's fine. I'm looking after it for a friend." And before too long, it had eaten the slug all up, and was sitting grooming its feathers as if nothing had happened.

"Oh look, you've scratched your neck," Shirley said, "let me dress it for you."

So far as she could tell, the wound was clean, "this will sting a little," she said dabbing some alcohol on it, then adding a dressing.

Fingers crossed it would be fine.

He watched the bird, as she shared the information she'd discovered, while she watched him, looking for any evidence something of the slug had remained behind.

"How do you feel?" she asked when she'd finished.

Derek frowned, "I'm a bit sad about the guy driving the car. The death of his wife and child must have been eating away at him, and I know how that feels."

She made an encouraging noise.

"But I feel like I've wasted the last few years. My kids are strangers to me now, and it'll take some work to regain their trust.

"But I know it will be worth it. And thanks to you, my wife will welcome me back. And my boss too."

"I'm glad," she said.

It seemed safe to let him go.

The next day, she and Edward visited the other houses with grief slug infestations, taking the strudel and the chicken with them.

One by one, they watched the slug disarmed by the strudel, and dismembered by the chicken.

All in all, an exhausting yet satisfying day.

«« • »»

They sat on the balcony, enjoying a well-earned beer and watching the neighbourhood kids playing five-a-side soccer on the green.

"Good job Edward," she said, raising her glass to him.

"Good job Shirley," replied, raising his to her.

"Hope we never see those grief slugs again."

He shuddered delicately, "bloody hope not too."

One of the teams in the park scored a goal, and cheered and jumped and hugged each other.

"I was thinking Chinese to celebrate," she said.

"Don't you dare make any chicken jokes."

"Not Kung Pao?"

"No.

"Not General Tso's?

"No."

"Not Moo Goo Gai?"

"No."

"I've had enough of you and chicken for one day," he stood up, "I'm off."

She smiled, "see you tomorrow then," she said as he winked out.

An hour later, Jeremy arrived with more beer.

"Are you alone?" he asked, looking wildly about the room as if expecting a bogey man.

"He's gone. We're good. Did you bring the CD?"

He looked around, then pulled three out of his backpack. "*Invasion of the Body Snatchers*; 1956, 1978, and that weird 2007 version."

"Perfect. I got take out. Come upstairs where we can watch them in comfort."

They snuggled up on the couch as he queued the 1956 version.

"So, how was your day?" she asked

"Nothing much. You?"

"Same."

It was nice to take a break from the surreal now and again, but she wouldn't want to live there.

THE END

ABOUT THE AUTHOR

Alexandria Blaelock writes stories, some of them for *Ellery Queen's Mystery Magazine* and *Pulphouse Fiction Magazine.*

She's also written five self-help books applying business techniques to personal matters like getting dressed, cleaning house, and feeding your friends.

She lives in a forest because she enjoys birdsong, and the smell of gum leaves. When not telecommuting to parallel universes from her Melbourne based imagination, she watches K-dramas, talks to animals, and drinks Campari. At the same time.
Discover more at www.alexandriablaelock.com.

IF YOU ENJOYED THIS STORY...

... you might like the other Wilksinson's stories

 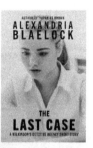

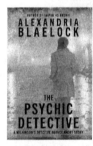 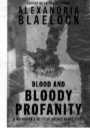 

... the whole collection

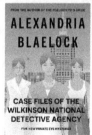

... or the first Georgia Garside

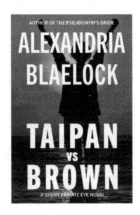

The Robin Hood of Private Investigators

Georgia Garside. Foul-mouthed Private
Investigator. Ex-contorionist.

Out of her depth. In over her head.

Caught up in the war between a wealthy
industrialist and the ex-sugar babe who can't take a
hint.

A laugh-out-loud tripartite battle of wits, winner
takes all.